Shadows of Rosalind Hollow

Shadows of Rosalind Hollow

Anurag Anurag

Anurag Anurag

1

The Quest for Truth

Sarah Carter, an intrepid investigative journalist driven by an insatiable thirst for uncovering untold stories, arrives in Rosalind Hollow propelled by an ambitious pursuit. Her reputation precedes her, marked by a history of unearthing concealed truths and shedding light on obscured narratives.

The allure of Rosalind Hollow, whispered to her through snippets of conversations and cryptic messages, beckons Sarah. A town steeped in enigma, its name synonymous with a legacy of secrets veiled beneath its charming facade, becomes the focal point of her relentless quest for the next breakthrough story.

The journey that brought Sarah to Rosalind Hollow traces back to a cryptic lead—whispers of something amiss within the town's tranquil veil. A mysterious source, wary yet determined to reveal the concealed truths, had cautiously extended an invitation, hinting at the depths of hidden stories nestled within the town's mist-laden streets.

Driven by an innate curiosity and an unyielding commitment to uncovering the obscured truths that resonate within Rosalind Hollow's soul, Sarah embarked on this investigative expedition. Her determination to peel back the layers of mystery and reveal the truth hidden within the town's enigmatic embrace fuels her every step.

As she steps foot into the quaint yet enigmatic enclave, Sarah's resolve solidifies. Her pursuit of truth becomes more than just a journalistic endeavor; it transforms into a personal quest to unravel the mysteries and unearth the concealed narratives that linger within the very fabric of Rosalind Hollow.

The Veil of Intrigue

As Sarah's boots touch the cobblestone streets of Rosalind Hollow, her arrival heralds the commencement of an odyssey entrenched in pursuit of the town's buried secrets. A glint of fierce determination, camouflaged by a veneer of professional composure, gleams in her piercing eyes—an unwavering resolve to unearth the concealed truths entrenched within the town's obscured annals.

Mayor Thomas, an emblem of polished charm and calculated affability, extends a warm embrace cloaked in calculated hospitality. Concealed beneath his geniality lies a guarded agenda—a protector of Rosalind Hollow's enigmatic mysteries. His eyes, cordial yet shrouded in watchfulness, recognize the peril Sarah's relentless probing might pose to the town's closely-guarded enigmas.

Emily, the seemingly amiable waitress of the local diner, greets Sarah with a studied smile that thinly veils her internal conflict. Behind the façade of warmth resides an undercurrent of apprehension, hints of a life entangled within the town's labyrinthine secrets. Each word she shares with Sarah carries the weight of concealed truths, careful phrases woven into tales that flutter on the edge of disclosure.

In the periphery, Nathan, the enigmatic artist, maintains a silent vigil, his keen gaze veiled by the shadows. His solitary disposition mirrors the mystery that cloaks Rosalind Hollow. Sarah's arrival captures his attention, yet the motives behind his guarded curiosity remain an inscrutable puzzle—his silent observations a testament to an allegiance whose contours evade detection within the town's intricate tapestry.

Sarah finds reprieve from her inquiries within the aging confines of the guesthouse, where a haunting atmosphere envelops the surroundings. The mist-laden streets whisper ancient legends, evoking a thirst for truth that tingles in the air—a quest compelling enough to face the perils it may summon. Sarah remains resolute, poised to unravel the enigmas shrouding Rosalind Hollow, regardless of the shadows it might cast upon her path.

3

୬୶

Immersed in Enigma

Sarah's investigative senses ignite as she immerses herself in the enigmatic embrace of Rosalind Hollow. Each conversation with the locals

becomes a breadcrumb leading deeper into the town's labyrinth of secrets. Fragments of a concealed past surface whispered anecdotes painting a mosaic of mystery that shrouds the town's enigma in further obscurity.

Mayor Thomas, with his calculated warmth, becomes an enigmatic guide through the web of the town's secrets. His charm subtly veils a cautionary undercurrent, gently redirecting Sarah's inquiries away from certain avenues. Each deflected question adds another layer to the town's enigma, leaving Sarah to question the mayor's motivations.

Emily, the seemingly familiar face, weaves a complex tapestry of warmth intertwined with guarded reservation. Her demeanor fluctuates, hinting at deeper secrets concealed behind her hesitant smile. Sarah senses a reluctance to divulge, each interaction with Emily stirring more questions than answers.

Nathan's solitary existence and cryptic artistry serve as haunting echoes of Rosalind Hollow's obscured history. His enigmatic creations seem to mirror the town's hidden truths, drawing Sarah into a web of symbolism and mystery. The artist's silence speaks volumes, leaving Sarah to wonder about the secrets buried within his solitary world.

As Sarah delves deeper into the town's layers, the thin veneer of normalcy peels away, revealing a labyrinth of shadows concealing buried truths. Intrigue crackles in the air, the palpable tension pushing Sarah to the precipice of revelation. The tantalizing prospect of uncovering the town's secrets feels within reach yet remains frustratingly elusive, dangling just beyond her grasp.

4

∽

Veiled Whispers

Sarah's insatiable curiosity about Rosalind Hollow's hidden history
grows with each passing day. The town's antiquated charm conceals a

deeper, ominous undercurrent. Mr. Beaumont, the enigmatic owner of an antique shop, speaks in cryptic riddles that only deepen the mystery. His cautionary words hint at dangerous paths Sarah's investigation might tread.

A chance discovery—a weathered journal wrapped in a faded cloth—adds fuel to Sarah's quest. Its cryptic contents, written in an ancient script, hint at a forgotten language and a connection to the town's past. Nathan's unexpected interest in the journal sparks a brief yet revealing conversation, leaving Sarah with more questions than answers.

Late one evening, a shadowy figure delivers an ominous message at Sarah's doorstep, urging caution in her pursuit of the town's secrets. Each revelation seems to unravel a new layer of intrigue, leaving Sarah teetering on the brink of an enigma she's determined to unravel.

Sarah's dedication to deciphering the journal's cryptic contents consumes her. Each faded page holds secrets that seem intertwined with the very essence of Rosalind Hollow. The weathered parchment, adorned with ancient symbols and intricate script, reads like a whispered echo from a distant era. Nathan, the taciturn artist, inadvertently aids Sarah's quest through his haunting paintings, which bear an uncanny resemblance to the symbols she's unraveling.

As Sarah delves deeper, the fragmented lines of the journal seem to weave a tale of an ancient ritual, invoking images of an otherworldly connection between the town's forgotten past and its enigmatic present. The lines between reality and myth blur as Sarah's investigation converges with the eerily familiar symbols from Nathan's enigmatic art.

The town's misty veil seems to part, revealing glimpses of a truth Sarah can't yet grasp—a revelation teetering on the edge of her understanding. However, before she can piece together the last fragments of the puzzle, a shadowy figure materializes from the town's enigmatic depths. Their presence, shrouded in ominous warnings, sends ripples of apprehension through Sarah's relentless pursuit of the town's enigmatic secrets.

5

The Conspiracies Unveiled

The morning sun rose over Rosalind Hollow, casting an ethereal glow upon the town's aged facades. Sarah's quest for truth intensified as she delved deeper into the town's enigmatic past, driven by an unrelenting curiosity that bordered on obsession.

The symbols from the mysterious journal haunted her thoughts, each line etched with an arcane significance that eluded comprehension. A chance encounter led her to Elias, a somber figure with a haunting gaze, once an Arbiter but now disillusioned by the group's secrets.

Elias hesitated, his voice tinged with remorse, "You tread dangerous paths, Ms. Carter. The Arbiters have wielded unseen influence for generations, their veiled actions entwined with power and deception."

Arbiters—an obscure collective hidden within the town's depths, cloaked in shadows, their actions shrouded in secrecy. Sarah's investigations had unveiled a connection between The Arbiters and Rosalind Hollow's influential figures, hinting at a sinister conspiracy woven into the town's very fabric.

Guided by Elias's cryptic warnings, Sarah delved deeper into the labyrinth of secrets, uncovering clandestine meetings and covert dealings orchestrated by The Arbiters. Her determination to unearth the truth propelled her further into a perilous web of intrigue.

A faded photograph, tucked away in the attic of an abandoned house, revealed a nexus of connections—a young Sage, the librarian, alongside key figures from the town's history, each obscured in the shadows of a forgotten era.

The sinister implications of The Arbiters' influence weighed heavily on Sarah's mind. A clandestine meeting between the town's mayor and the group's enigmatic leader, identified only by a moniker—The Whisperer—etched doubts into her consciousness.

As dusk settled upon Rosalind Hollow, the town's secrets danced tantalizingly close, yet remained frustratingly elusive. Sarah teetered on the precipice of unveiling a conspiracy entwined with power, deceit, and the darkest depths of the human psyche.

6

Dangerous Pursuits

Sarah's relentless pursuit of truth unwittingly garners the attention of shadowy entities deeply entrenched within Rosalind Hollow's enigmatic tapestry. The unnerving sense of being watched morphs into an unshakeable presence, manifesting in unnerving incidents—a rustle in the dense foliage, fleeting figures vanishing at the corner of her gaze. The once-charming cobblestone streets now resonate with an ominous hollowness, each footfall echoing through an eerie, haunting silence.

What begins as an ordinary venture into the town's bustling market transmutes into a nerve-wracking escapade. The vibrant bazaar turns into a silent stage for a harrowing pursuit. Elusive figures dart amidst stalls, their obscured forms a foreboding testament to a lurking peril. Sarah's breath quickens, the adrenaline coursing through her veins, amplifying the dissonance between her racing pulse and the unnerving stillness surrounding her.

The chase through Rosalind Hollow's alleys is a nerve-wracking labyrinth, the narrow pathways snaking between centuries-old buildings draped in tendrils of mist. Sarah's breath quickens as she dashes around corners, her heart pounding in sync with her footsteps echoing against cobblestone streets. The eerie silence amplifies the sounds of her hurried flight, broken only by the occasional rustle of leaves disturbed by the wind or the distant hoot of an owl.

The alleys, once familiar by daylight, now transform into a maze of uncertainty as the mist weaves illusions, playing tricks on her perception. Shadows dance along the walls, morphing into elusive, enigmatic figures that vanish as quickly as they appear. Sarah's senses strain against the shroud of fog, her pulse racing as she navigates this nocturnal puzzle, her instincts her only guide through the obscure pathways.

As she races deeper into the heart of the town, the looming structures seem to lean closer, casting elongated shadows that reach out like ghostly fingers. Each turn intensifies the feeling of being watched, an unnerving sensation that pricks at the edges of her consciousness. The air grows colder, thick with the weight of secrets long held within Rosalind Hollow's history.

In this haunting backdrop, the pursuit escalates into a heart-stopping confrontation. Sarah, her back pressed against an ancient stone wall, stands breathless, her chest rising and falling in rapid succession. Across from her, a cloaked figure materializes from the mist, an enigmatic silhouette exuding an ominous aura. The tension crackles in the air, a palpable force that renders the surroundings eerily still.

In the mist-laden alleys of Rosalind Hollow, Sarah finds herself ensnared in an intense confrontation with shadowy, masked figures. These enigmatic beings, veiled in secrecy and emitting an eerie sense of threat, stand as guardians of the town's hidden truths. Initially charmed by Rosalind Hollow's quaint exterior, Sarah now faces its darker underbelly through this chilling encounter.

The standoff unfolds in a charged silence. Sarah confronts these figures, their faces obscured by masks that betray no emotion. Eyes hidden behind the enigmatic coverings communicate volumes, laden with unspoken warnings and a veiled sense of menace. The mist swirls around them, almost as if the atmosphere itself is privy to the ancient mysteries concealed within the town.

As the tension thickens, Sarah grapples with an overwhelming urge to unravel the secrets lurking within Rosalind Hollow's tapestry. The figures, custodians of these enigmatic truths, hold their ground with an impenetrable facade, maintaining a silence that leaves Sarah teetering on the precipice of an unknown abyss.

In this charged moment, the weight of the town's clandestine past hangs heavy in the air, enveloping Sarah in a palpable sense of anticipation. The standoff becomes a crucial juncture, where Sarah's pursuit of truth collides head-on with the guardians of Rosalind Hollow's mysteries.

The standoff lingers, an unspoken challenge echoing through the mist-filled streets. The intricate web of enigmatic secrets tightens its grip, leaving Sarah on the brink of a revelation that promises to reshape her investigative journey to its core. The charged atmosphere holds the promise of unveiling the town's concealed truths, yet Sarah remains poised on the edge, caught between uncovering the enigma and succumbing to the foreboding unknown.

7

Unveiling the Clandestine Archives

Embraced by the alliance of Elias and Lila, Sarah plunges headlong into a relentless quest to decode the cryptic relics extracted from Rosalind Hollow's clandestine archives. Each ancient tome and faded parchment holds fragments of a history veiled by centuries, whispering tales of a clandestine society—the enigmatic Arbiters—entwined with the very essence of the town's existence.

Elias, initially hesitant, reluctantly guides Sarah into the shadowy world of the Arbiters. Glimpses of secretive meetings and the obscured influence wielded by this clandestine group emerge hesitantly from his lips. His revelations hint at the veiled power and intricate machinations orchestrated by the enigmatic society, painting a tantalizing but treacherous path into the town's hidden history.

Meanwhile, Lila, armed with technological prowess, becomes an indispensable ally in deciphering the archaic symbols and penetrating the cryptic codes guarding the town's darkest truths. Her mastery over deciphering ancient enigmas complements Elias's insights, forming a trifecta of expertise that edges closer to unlocking the town's enigmatic past.

The collaborative efforts of Sarah, Elias, and Lila propel them deeper into the enigmatic heart of Rosalind Hollow's obscured history. Their tireless pursuit yields a wealth of revelations as they decode the cryptic relics within the clandestine archives.

The ancient script, once an inscrutable labyrinth of symbols, gradually unravels under their collective scrutiny. As the trio delves into the intricacies of the text, hidden truths begin to emerge, painting a portrait of the Arbiters' clandestine activities throughout the town's history.

In their decipherment, they uncover fragmented accounts of the Arbiters' manipulations—a trove of historical events influenced and manipulated by this clandestine society. References to covert meetings and obscured dealings hint at the group's intricate involvement in shaping Rosalind Hollow's fate.

Sarah, Elias, and Lila uncover instances where the Arbiters exploited the town's resources for personal gain. Veiled references suggest the group's hand in orchestrating events to serve their clandestine objectives, manipulating the town's trajectory and affecting the lives of its inhabitants across generations.

Furthermore, the ancient script alludes to power struggles and concealed motivations woven into Rosalind Hollow's historical fabric. Clues buried within the texts reveal a web of secrets—covert influences and obscured agendas—that resonate through the annals of time, tainting the town's once-idyllic narrative.

As each cryptic passage yields its secrets, the trio finds themselves entrenched in an enigmatic history where the line between truth and deception blurs. The weight of their discoveries amplifies, drawing them deeper into the labyrinth of secrets that define the obscured tapestry of Rosalind Hollow.

8

~

Betrayals and Twists

Sarah, Elias, and Lila find themselves entrenched in an increasingly convoluted web of mysteries, but fissures begin to fracture their once-united front. Cryptic messages, seemingly innocuous gestures, and veiled conversations gradually erode the foundation of trust that had bound them together.

Elias, the enigmatic informant turned ally, adopts a guarded demeanor, his usual transparency veiled by a newfound secrecy. Sarah's attempts to discern the reason behind his sudden change hit an impenetrable wall. Meanwhile, Lila, once a steadfast companion in their pursuit of truth, seems to harbor obscured intentions. Her actions, once unquestionable, now cast shadows of doubt on her motives.

As the trio navigates through the labyrinth of Rosalind Hollow's mysteries, unsettling revelations surface, breeding paranoia and confusion. Conflicting loyalties come to light, and betrayals unfold amidst their tangled alliances. Sarah finds herself grappling with an unnerving realization—every relationship she forged in the pursuit of truth might have been shrouded in hidden agendas.

Betrayals cut deep, isolating Sarah and leaving her vulnerable in a treacherous landscape where deceit reigns supreme. The intricate layers of hidden motives and conflicting interests erode the once-solid foundation of trust, forcing her to confront a harsh truth—everyone she trusted might have harbored their secrets, each alliance masking ulterior motives beneath a facade of camaraderie.

With the bonds of trust shattered, Sarah is left to navigate the treacherous terrain of Rosalind Hollow's mysteries alone, haunted by the echoes of broken alliances and the realization that she stands on shifting sands, unsure of who to trust in her relentless pursuit of the elusive truth.

9

Revealing Rosalind's Secrets

The obscured history of the Arbiters isn't merely a matter of historical curiosity but a pivotal element that entwines itself with the town's present and future. Sarah's quest to disclose the secrets of the Arbiters is rooted in the understanding that these revelations could hold the key to critical aspects that affect the town's stability:

- Economic Stability: The Arbiters' historical manipulation of resources might have lingering effects on Rosalind Hollow's economy. If these secrets reveal exploitative practices or resource mismanagement, it could impact the town's financial stability.
- Social Fabric: The group's historical influence might have seeded divisions or biases among the townspeople. Uncovering these truths could either exacerbate existing tensions or pave the way for healing past wounds.
- Political Impact: The Arbiters' clandestine meetings and manipulations likely influenced political decisions across history. Exposing these influences could shake the town's political structure, causing instability or leading to reforms.
- Existential Threat: Sarah suspects that the Arbiters' past actions may hold clues to an impending catastrophe. If left unaddressed, this catastrophe could pose an existential threat to Rosalind Hollow, whether it's environmental, social, or another form of impending disaster.

The ancient script, encoded with historical secrets, serves as a clandestine repository—a cryptic testament to the obscured truths woven into Rosalind Hollow's enigmatic history. Its existence is a testament to the clandestine nature of the Arbiters, who meticulously concealed their manipulative exploits within the town's very fabric.

Sarah's urgency stems from her realization that the revelations encapsulated within the script hold profound significance for the town's well-being. The secrets buried within these ancient texts are more than mere historical accounts; they are keys to unlocking a legacy of manipulation, exploitation, and impending catastrophe lurking in the shadows.

Each piece of the cryptic puzzle, painstakingly deciphered by the trio, represents a fragment of the Arbiters' clandestine operations. These historical secrets, concealed within the script, encapsulate the group's covert influences, exploitative actions, and obscured motives that echo through Rosalind Hollow's annals.

Sarah's pursuit isn't merely fueled by curiosity; it's a race against time to prevent an imminent disaster foretold by the ancient revelations. Her belief in the potential impact of these historical truths on the town's trajectory drives her relentless pursuit. She understands that these hidden secrets hold the key to averting a calamity looming within the shadows—an impending catastrophe shrouded in the town's enigmatic past.

With every deciphered fragment, Sarah inches closer to piecing together the puzzle that could potentially alter Rosalind Hollow's course. The urgency in her pursuit intensifies, driven by the realization that the town's fate hinges on unraveling these enigmatic historical secrets before the looming disaster descends upon the tranquil enclave.

10

∾

The Race Against Time

Sarah's revelation about the Arbiters' catastrophic plans plunges Rosalind Hollow into a menacing shadow of imminent peril. Determined

to halt the impending disaster, she plunges into a pulse-pounding race against the relentless march of time.

The weight of responsibility bears down heavily on Sarah as she navigates the treacherous landscape of the Arbiters' intricate schemes. Each step forward feels like a perilous dance on the edge of catastrophe, uncertainty clouding every decision.

Confronting the Arbiters, their sinister presence radiates a chilling aura, casting a pall over the impending showdown. Unseen dangers echo through the town, intensifying the already palpable tension. Veiled threats and cryptic warnings lace the air, heightening the nerve-wracking anticipation of an inevitable clash.

The urgency propels Sarah into the heart of the impending catastrophe, where the fate of Rosalind Hollow hangs in a delicate balance. Every heartbeat is a race against the clock, each breath fueling her determination to avert the looming disaster and protect the town from an unfathomable fate.

In a gripping showdown, Sarah faces off against the Arbiters, each move and decision a gambit in the high-stakes battle for the town's survival. The pulse of impending catastrophe beats louder with each passing moment, leaving Sarah standing at the precipice, knowing that the fate of Rosalind Hollow and its inhabitants rests upon her shoulders.

The Final Showdown

Sarah stands at the precipice of an epic reckoning as she faces off against The Whisperer, the elusive mastermind behind the Arbiters.

Startling truths emerge, reshaping her understanding of Rosalind Hollow's intricate web of events and characters entangled within it.

In a suspenseful confrontation, The Whisperer's identity is unveiled, exposing their pivotal role in orchestrating the Arbiters' clandestine operations. Revelations cascade forth, revealing the extent of the Arbiters' illegal activities, including, Manipulation of town resources for personal gain. Fabrication of historical events to suit their agenda. Covert interventions in political and social affairs, shaping the town's course for centuries.

Sarah's unrelenting pursuit of truth culminates in an intense showdown that brings the Arbiters' misdeeds to light. As the town grapples with these revelations, a wave of indignation sweeps through Rosalind Hollow. The exp osure of the Arbiters' illegal activities ignites public outcry, demanding justice for their manipulative actions. Community leaders and legal authorities rally to take action.

Consequently, investigations ensue, uncovering evidence validating Sarah's discoveries. Legal measures are initiated, leading to the prosecution of key members of the Arbiters involved in the illicit operations. The legal consequences serve as a landmark moment for justice, as those accountable face penalties for their misdeeds.

The town undergoes a transformative phase, marked by introspection and reform. Rosalind Hollow collectively addresses the aftermath of the Arbiters' exposure: Reforms in governance and local policies ensure transparency and accountability. Community-driven initiatives foster unity and healing, aiming to mend the societal divides sowed by the Arbiters' manipulations. A newfound spirit of resilience and unity permeates through the town, fostering a renewed sense of trust among its inhabitants.

Sarah's tireless pursuit not only exposes the Arbiters' dark secrets but catalyzes a transformative chapter in Rosalind Hollow's history. The town embarks on a journey of recovery and progress, learning from its past and embracing a brighter future built on truth and integrity.

12

꙰

Redemption and Renewal

Sarah stands amid the aftermath of the seismic revelations that shook Rosalind Hollow to its core. The exposure of the Arbiters' clandestine operations and subsequent legal actions have reshaped the town's landscape. As she prepares to bid farewell to the enigmatic town, echoes of its secrets continue to reverberate.

The investigations following the exposure of the Arbiters' illegal activities yield concrete evidence. Key members of the group, responsible for orchestrating manipulative schemes, face the consequences of their misdeeds. Legal trials unfold, marking a pivotal moment where justice is served. High-profile figures implicated in the Arbiters' schemes are held accountable, facing penalties commensurate with their actions.

The repercussions ripple through Rosalind Hollow. The town, once shrouded in shadows of deceit, now emerges into the light of truth and accountability. Governance undergoes a transformation, rooted in transparency and ethical practices. The community unites in collective introspection, determined to heal the wounds inflicted by years of covert manipulation.

Public initiatives are launched, fostering unity and rebuilding the societal fabric frayed by the Arbiters' machinations. Town hall meetings resonate with impassioned discussions, driving reforms aimed at preventing such deceitful influences in the future. Citizens actively participate in shaping the town's new narrative, ensuring that the mistakes of the past serve as lessons for a more resilient future.

Sarah's departure marks the closure of a chapter in Rosalind Hollow's history. Her quest for truth not only unveiled the town's darkest secrets but instigated a cathartic purge of deceit. As she bids farewell to the town she meticulously unraveled, Rosalind Hollow stands on the precipice of a new era.

The once-veiled town is now a testament to resilience, reclaiming its identity built on honesty and integrity. Sarah, a catalyst for change, leaves behind a legacy of courage and relentless pursuit of justice, her impact woven into the fabric of Rosalind Hollow's rebirth.

As she journeys away from the town's mist-laden streets, Sarah carries with her the echoes of its secrets—secrets that shaped her, challenged her, and ultimately led her to be a harbinger of truth.